The
WEREWOLF
Hunter's Guide

Ursula Lestrade

SEA-TO-SEA
Mankato Collingwood London

Imagine yourself heading home along a lonely street one night. Behind you, you hear the tip-tap of clawed feet on concrete. It's probably a stray dog, or perhaps a raccoon, finding its way by the light of the full moon. Or maybe... it's a werewolf, a human who has been **transformed** by the moonlight into a flesh-ripping fiend!

If you DO meet a werewolf on your way home from school, what should you do? This book tells you everything you need to know: how to recognize different kinds of werewolf, methods of escape, and even how to destroy one.

Good luck!

Ursula Lestrade

INSIDE...

4   Werewolves All Around!

6   Werewolf Characteristics

8   The Legend of Sigmund and Sinfjotli

10   Pricolici of Romania

12   Vilkacis of Latvia and Lithuania

14   The Jura Werewolves

16   The Skinwalkers of North America

18   Rougarou of Louisiana

20   The Beast of Bray Road

22   Lobisomem of Brazil

24   The Benandanti Werewolves

26   Werewolves at the Movies

28   Other Man Beasts

30   Technical Information

31   More Werewolf Information

32   Index

Words in bold are in the glossary.

Werewolves All Around!

Many legends tell of werewolves that look like ordinary people by day. It is only at night that their true form is revealed. Their bodies are gripped with the werewolf **curse** as they change into bloodthirsty killers.

Worldwide Threat

Today, werewolves have spread around the world. Almost anywhere you go, you will hear stories of **shapeshifting** humans who become wolflike when the moon is full. Not all werewolves are evil killers. Some do no harm. But their bloodthirsty **kindred** more than make up for these peaceable werewolves.

▼ Werewolves have featured in many movies over the years.

The CURSE OF THE WEREWOLF

in Eastman COLOR

Starring CLIFFORD EVANS · OLIVER REED · YVONNE ROMAIN · CATHERINE FELLER

Screenplay by JOHN ELDER Directed by TERENCE FISHER Produced by ANTHONY HINDS Executive Producer MICHAEL CARRERAS

Werewolf Hunter's Kit

No sensible werewolf hunter would be without the following weapons:

• Silver weapons kill werewolves. Silver swords and bullets are particularly good.

• Wolfbane, a plant that

Silver weapons and bullets

4

▲ This unlucky traveler has met with a werewolf. Now, he will never reach home.

The Werewolf Hunters

All that stands between ferocious killer werewolves and normal people is a select band of werewolf hunters. They know how werewolves act, the danger signs that indicate that one is nearby, and the best ways to destroy a werewolf. This guide contains their secrets. Reading it is your first step to becoming a werewolf hunter.

grows around the world. It is poisonous to humans, as well as werewolves.

• Plants such as rye and mistletoe, and berries from the mountain ash tree are also said to safeguard against werewolf attack.

Mistletoe

Mountain ash berries

Wolfbane

Werewolf Characteristics

Werewolves appear in different forms. A good werewolf hunter must be able to recognize all of them.

Recognizing Werewolves

The following are some of the clues that someone may be a werewolf:

• Their eyebrows meet in the middle.

• They have red hair, or have hairs growing on the palms of their hands.

• If their skin is cut open, there will be fur underneath it.

• They love raw or barely cooked meat.

• They were born on Christmas Day.

Some werewolves look like wolves once they have been transformed. Other werewolves look more like a cross between a wolf and a human. Many stories suggest that the change from human to werewolf is triggered by the full moon.

▼ *A night lit by a full moon. This is the time of each month when you are most likely to meet a werewolf.*

▼ This werewolf is a terrifying cross between a wolf and a human.

Key Werewolf Characteristics

Whatever form they take, all werewolves have some things in common:

- They are unbelievably strong.
- They can run long distances at speed, and climb high walls with ease.
- In wolf form, they have no tail, and keep their human eyes and voice.

Some werewolves are **immune** to ordinary weapons (though never to silver bullets), and can only be killed when in human form.

The Werewolf's Bite

The usual way for people to become a werewolf is to be bitten by one. Most people who are bitten by a werewolf die, of course. But if they survive, they will become a werewolf.

HOW WEREWOLVES ARE MADE

The usual way for people to become a werewolf is being bitten by one. But there are plenty of other ways to become a werewolf:

- Being cursed by a witch or magician.
- Being smeared with a special potion.
- Falling asleep outdoors with the full moon shining on your face on a Wednesday or Friday.

7

The Legend of Sigmund and Sinfjotli

The legend of Sigmund and Sinfjotli comes from the frozen lands of the North.

Werewolf Fact File

Name: Varulfur
Location: Iceland
Age: at least 500 years

One day, Sigmund and Sinfjotli were out hunting and found a cabin with two men asleep inside. Next to the sleepers lay two large wolf skins. The skins looked so fine and warm Sigmund and Sinfjotli crept forward, and tried them on. Too late, they realized their mistake! The skins were cursed to transform the wearer into a wolf.

A Promise

The curse of the skins lasts for nine days. Until then, Sigmund and Sinfjotli must survive as wolves. They decide to separate, but each promises to come if the other is attacked or hunted by men.

▼ Many werewolf stories come from the snowy lands of Iceland and Scandinavia.

▲ *The cursed skins transform Sigmund and Sinfjotli into howling wolves.*

Hunted

Sigmund and Sinfjotli's promise is soon put to the test. When a group of hunters pursue Sigmund, he howls out to Sinfjotli for help. Sinfjotli races to his aid, and together they kill every hunter. But then more hunters appear. Sinfjotli is pursued by 11 men, but he doesn't call his friend for help. Instead, he kills them all himself.

Werewolf Fight!

When Sigmund discovers what has happened, he asks why Sinfjotli did not call for help. Sinfjotli replies arrogantly that—unlike Sigmund—he did not need any help. Furious, Sigmund attacks, biting Sinfjotli in the throat. Then, **wracked** with guilt, he carries Sinfjotli back to the cabin in the woods. As he arrives, a raven brings him a magical plant, which heals Sinfjotli's wounds.

By now, the nine days are up, and the werewolf curse has lifted. Instead of leaving the skins for others to find, Sigmund and Sinfjotli burn them—ensuring there are two fewer werewolves than before.

9

Pricolici of Romania

The mountains of Romania can be dangerous territory. Many strange and deadly creatures survive there, such as the pricolici. Pricolici are werewolves, but have many vampire **traits**.

Werewolf Fact File

Name: Pricolici
Location: Central Europe
Age: First recorded in 1716

Pricolici Behavior

Pricolici are the remains of humans who are dead and buried, but rise up from their graves at night. They take the shape of wolves. Pricolici attack the living silently and—with terrible violence—drink their blood and eat their flesh.

▼ *If you visit the lonely, inhospitable valleys of Central Europe, beware—there may be pricolici on the prowl here.*

> "All werewolves are of evil disposition, having assumed a **bestial** form to satisfy a bestial appetite... for human flesh."
>
> –Ambrose Bierce (1842-1914)

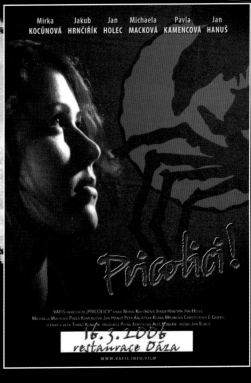

Mirka KOCÚNOVÁ Jakub HRNČIŘÍK Jan HOLEC Michaela MACKOVÁ Pavla KAMENCOVÁ Jan HANUŠ

Pricolici!

VAFIS uvádí film „PRICOLICI" hrají Mirka Kocúnová Jakub Hrnčiřík Jan Holec Michaela Macková Pavla Kamencová Jan Hanuš Petr Andrýsek Klára Mišunová Christopher J. Grippo scénář a režie Tomáš Kopečný producent Petra Jiřičková Aleš Pivařík hudba Jan Buros

16. 3. 2006
restaurace Oáza

WWW.VAFIS.INFO/FILM

► *Bloodthirsty pricolici feature in many Romanian horror movies.*

Discovering Pricolici

It is said that if the grave of a pricolici is dug up, it will be found lying face down with its rear in the air, and will have blood on its lips. This blood, if given to any of the pricolici's victims who are still alive, will make them well again, and will take away the werewolf curse.

▼ *An old graveyard in Romania. Could one of these headstones have a pricolici sheltering beneath it?*

Fighting and Destroying

Because they have so much in common with vampires, pricolici can be fought and destroyed in the same ways:

• A stake through the heart.
• A silver bullet.
• Cutting off their head and stuffing their mouth with garlic.

Some stories also say that if pricolici are caught out of their grave during daylight, they will be destroyed.

Vilkacis of Latvia and Lithuania

In northern Europe, on the shores of the cold Baltic Sea, are the lands of Latvia and Lithuania. This bleak, windswept country is home to the vilkacis, which are among Europe's oldest werewolves.

Werewolf Fact File

Name: Vilkacis (male), vilkatas (female)
Location: Latvia and Lithuania
Age: several hundred years

What Is a Vilkacis?

Most people say that vilkacis are humans who turn into wolves. A few people say they are people who can transport their souls into the body of a wolf. However the transformation happens, most stories agree that the vilkacis is more likely to attack animals such as cattle or sheep than humans.

◄ *Could this snarling wolf in fact be a vilkacis?*

Becoming a Vilkacis

Being bitten by a vilkacis is a sure way to become one yourself, but it's not the only one. There are at least two other ways in which people can become a vilkacis:

- When the moon is full, sleep under a tree whose tip has curled down to touch the earth.
- Wrap yourself in a wolf's skin and say an **incantation.**

Vilkacis are unusual among werewolves, because they have no special powers or protection. They can be shot or gotten rid of in the same way as ordinary wolves.

TRAPPED AS A WOLF

Some stories say that when women become vilkatas, they must leave their clothes hidden where no one can find them. If the clothes are touched while the woman is in wolf form, she will not be able to become human again. Instead, she is cursed to stay a wolf for nine years.

▼ *A vilkacis in the middle of transformation.*

The Jura Werewolves

This story is the tragic case of the Gandillon family. They lived more than 400 years ago in the mountainous Jura region, on the border between France and Switzerland. Almost the entire family were infected with the werewolf curse— with terrible **consequences**.

▼ The thick forests and steep valleys of the Jura region make ideal hunting grounds for werewolves.

An Attack

One day, two small children were attacked by a wolf in a forest in Jura. One of the children cut the wolf with a knife, and it fled. A group of hunters was soon on the wolf's trail, but when they found it, they got a terrible surprise.

The First Werewolf

What the hunters found was no wolf, but a young woman named Pernette Gandillon. She was covered in blood, and cut in the same place as the wolf had been. Soon afterward, a crowd of angry villagers **lynched** Pernette, convinced she was a werewolf.

▲ The Gandillons were able to transform themselves into wolves at will, and struck fear into local families with their brutal attacks.

More Gandillon Werewolves

Soon after Pernette's death, her sister, brother, and nephew were arrested. The sister quickly admitted she was a witch. The two men began to behave very strangely. They started to run about their cell on all fours, snarling and barking at people. They confessed to being Devil-worshiping werewolves.

Since Devil worship, being a werewolf, and witchcraft were all punishable by death, there could only be one outcome. All three surviving Gandillons were burned alive.

WEREWOLF TRANSFORMATION

The Gandillons claimed to become werewolves using a special potion they obtained from the Devil. They rubbed it on their skin to become wolves. To return to human form, they rolled in damp grass until the potion had been removed.

The Skinwalkers of North America

Imagine yourself out in the wilds of North America. Suddenly, you're aware of a wolf, traveling along beside you. But there's something strange about it. Is it a wolf—or could it be a skinwalker?

Werewolf Fact File

Name: Skinwalkers
Location: North America
Age: Several hundred years

◄ Skinwalkers get their name because they steal the "skin" of their victim. This skinwalker has stolen a human skin.

Skinwalker Characteristics

Skinwalkers are humans who can shape shift into an animal form, usually a coyote or wolf. They can read human minds and copy human voices.

Detection and Destruction

In its human form, it is almost impossible to spot a skinwalker. The only way is to track the creature in its animal form back to its home. Skinwalkers, like other werewolves, will have the same injuries as the animal version—this can be a way of identifying them.

In animal form, it is easy to spot a skinwalker. They cannot walk in the same way as a real animal because they are less agile. The Navajo say you can destroy a skinwalker if you find out its human identity. Call out the skinwalker's human name, and then say, "You are a skinwalker!" Within three days it will be dead.

PROTECTION AGAINST SKINWALKERS

Protect yourself against attack by a skinwalker by covering your body with one of the following:
- The ash of a cedar tree,
- The juice of juniper berries,
- Corn pollen (but it's very tricky to collect!).

▶ *The skinwalker's favorite animal form is the coyote.*

Rougarou of Louisiana

In southern Louisiana lie the "Bottoms." These misty, damp swamplands are mysterious places. Poisonous snakes and alligators are not the only dangers here—this is where rougarou hunts for his victims.

Werewolf Fact File

Name: Rougarou
Location: southern Louisiana
Age: several hundred years

▼ *You are in the greatest danger of meeting a rougarou in swampy wetlands like this.*

Detection

Rougarou is a werewolf, with a terrible hunger for human flesh. As with so many werewolves, it is difficult to tell a rougarou from a normal person during the day.

One sign can be that someone is always very tired because they have been hunting for victims at night. After dark, rougarou takes on his werewolf form. He has a human body, but the head of a wolf.

People become rougarou by being bitten by a rougarou. Once infected, it is impossible to shed the werewolf curse during the first 101 days. On the 102nd day, the curse can be passed on by biting someone else.

Killing Rougarou

Some stories say that rougarou can only be killed by burning it or by cutting off its head. In its human form, rougarou can be killed the same way as any human being.

▲ *If you hear howling in the swamps and there's a full moon—watch out! There's a rougarou nearby.*

RELIGIOUS ENFORCER

Many stories tell how rougarou seeks out bad Roman Catholics as his victims. If you don't stick to the rules of **Lent**, in particular, watch out for rougarou coming out of the swamp to get you!

The Beast of Bray Road

Around the time of the full moon, the residents of the little town of Elkhorn, in Wisconsin, are careful to lock their doors at night. They stick to brightly lit areas, and stay away from the woods. Why? They don't want to run into the Beast.

Werewolf Fact File

Name: The Beast
Location: Wisconsin and Illinois
Age: first reported 1936

The Beast has appeared many times since it was first seen in 1936. Most witnesses describe it as a large, wolflike creature that goes around on its hind legs. It is 6–8 feet (2–2.5 m) tall, and powerfully built. Judging from drawings by witnesses, there seems little doubt that the Beast is a werewolf.

▲ The story of the Beast has inspired a book.

THE
BEAST
OF BRAY ROAD
Tailing Wisconsin's Werewolf
Linda S. Godfrey

▶ An artist's impression of the Beast.

▲ *Most people agree that the Beast is almost certainly a werewolf.*

Danger to Humans

The Beast has not yet attacked and killed a human, but there have been several near misses. A typical encounter took place when two men in a car spotted a large creature in the road. As they got closer they realized it was the Beast. As one of them rolled down the window for a better look, the Beast attacked. The men sped off—but the car was raked down the side by powerful claws.

What Is The Beast?

There are several theories about what the Beast may be. The most popular is that it is a werewolf, and at least one witness claims to have seen the Beast transforming itself from wolf form. Among the other possibilities are three creatures from Native American mythology:

- Shunka wara'kin—a **mythical** creature like a cross between a wolf and a hyena that walks on its back legs.

- Amarok, a giant wolflike creature that tracks and kills anyone foolish enough to hunt alone at night.

- A skinwalker (see pages 16–17).

21

Lobisomem of Brazil

If there's one place a werewolf hunter really must visit at least once, it's the Brazilian town of Joanópolis. There are more werewolf sightings in Joanópolis than anywhere else in the world.

In Brazil, werewolves are known as lobisomem. They are hideous wolflike creatures, with razor-sharp teeth and glowing red eyes. What they desire above all else is raw meat.

Werewolf Fact File

Name: Lobisomem
Location: Brazil
Age: not known

▲ Turn a corner in the Brazilian city of Joanópolis late at night, and you might find a lobisomem lurking in your path...

Behavior and Characteristics

Lobisomem change into wolves when they arrive at a crossroads at midnight on a Friday. Unlike many other werewolves, they do not need a full moon. Most werewolf hunters agree that lobisomem can only take human form again by finding the same crossroads, again at midnight.

Becoming a Lobisomem

▲ Lobisomem mainly feed on dead animals, but if they meet a human they attack!

There are several ways of becoming a lobisomem:
• People say that the seventh child of the same sex born in a row will become a lobisomem.
• Others say that if the eighth child is a boy after seven girls, he will become a lobisomem.
• A lobisomem bite will transmit the werewolf curse.

Lobisomem are extremely difficult to kill in wolf form, though they can be destroyed using silver weapons.

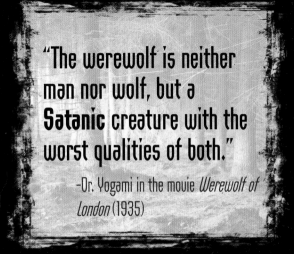

"The werewolf is neither man nor wolf, but a Satanic creature with the worst qualities of both."

−Dr. Yogami in the movie *Werewolf of London* (1935)

The Benandanti Werewolves

Werewolf Fact File

As a werewolf hunter, you become used to werewolves being your enemy. But there is another category of werewolf—the ones that actually fight evil.

Name: Benandanti
Location: Originally Italy
Age: at least 600 years

▲ A band of Benandanti head into battle, as a Malandanti witch swoops down to attack them.

Guardians

These werewolves are known as the Benandanti. For hundreds of years they have guarded the paths from the Underworld to the world of the living. Their special enemies are the Malandanti, a group of evil witches.

Benandanti Behavior

By day, the Benandanti look human, but at night their true nature is revealed. They transform into supernatural, wolflike creatures, in order to do battle with the forces of evil.

It is impossible to become a Benandanti by choice. You have to be born one. Membership does not run in families. Instead, it is a "gift" given to only a few people in each **generation**.

▶ *The Benandanti looked ferocious, but were, in fact, a force for good.*

Beware the False Benandanti

A careful werewolf hunter will be very wary of anyone claiming to be a Benandanti. Some time after about 1600, their sworn enemies, the witches, began to **infiltrate** the Benandanti ranks. The werewolves kept their identities hidden, and exist now only as a secret society. This means that anyone who openly claims to be a Benandanti is more likely to be a witch.

BATTLE WITH THE WITCHES

The Benandanti fight battles with witches on at least three nights of the year:
• St. Lucia's feast day, in midwinter.
• The Feast of St. John, in midsummer.
• Pentecost, in the harvest season.

Werewolves at the Movies

Werewolves have always been popular villains in horror movies. Recently, some have tried to show werewolves in a positive, romantic light. Do not be fooled! There are still plenty of bloodthirsty werewolves out there...

▲ Werewolves make terrifying villains in horror movies.

The Wolfman

The Wolfman (1941) was the movie that started the modern werewolf craze. It told the story of a man who is bitten when defending a woman from a werewolf. In the end, he becomes a werewolf himself, and has to be killed.

Underworld

The Underworld series of movies features a world where vampires and a species of werewolves called Lycans are deadly rivals. The Lycans were created when a wolf bit an immortal child. Spanning hundreds of years, the movies are set in a bleak, cheerless land.

Twilight

The *Twilight* movies center on the relationships between Bella Swan and the vampire Edward Cullen. But one of the key characters in the movies is the Native American Jacob Black, who is able to transform himself into a wolf. Jacob and other shapeshifting members of his tribe help rescue Bella from her enemies on several occasions.

"You really, honestly don't mind that I morph into a giant dog?"

– Jacob Black to Bella Swan in *New Moon*.

▼ *Bella is drawn to the mysterious shapeshifter Jacob Black in the* Twilight *movies.*

Other Man Beasts

As every werewolf hunter knows, werewolves aren't the only dangerous half-man, half-beasts you have to watch out for. Often a report of a werewolf turns out to be something else. These are just a few of the other monsters that appear from time to time.

"Those things out there are REAL. If they're real, what else is real? You know what lives in the shadows now. You may never get another night's sleep as long as you live."

– Megan, in the movie *The Dog Soldiers* (2002)

The Goatman

First sighted: 1957
Location: mainly Maryland, but as far south as Texas and as far north as Canada
With the legs of a goat, a man's upper body, and a horned head, the Goatman isn't difficult to identify. He has attacked several people, and is said to have killed many pets. His victims are often couples who have parked their car in **secluded** places.

▶ An artist's impression of the Goatman, who has been terrifying people in the United States and Canada for more than 50 years.

Momo

First sighted: July 1971
Location: Missouri

Momo is short for "Missouri Monster." Standing 7 feet (2.2 m) tall, and covered in thick, black fur, Momo is said to smell worse than garbage that's been rotting for a week. It is regularly reported to have eaten pet dogs, but has not yet attacked humans.

◀ *It's hard to be sure what's more unpleasant about Momo—the way he looks or the way he stinks!*

The Monkey Man

First sighted: 2001
Location: New Delhi, India

The Monkey Man is about 4 feet (1.2 m) tall, but is very strong and agile. He has attacked several people in New Delhi, in India, since 2001. Monkey Man has bitten and scratched people throughout the city, and is said to have caused at least two deaths as people fled from him in a panic.

▲ *Could this be India's mysterious Monkey Man?*

Technical Information

Words from this Book:

bestial
beastlike and disgusting

consequences
outcomes or results

curse
harm that is caused to someone by a supernatural power

generation
people born at around the same time

immune
unable to be harmed by something

incantation
spell or charm

infiltrate
become part of a group

kindred
members of the same family

Lent
forty days leading up to Easter, when some Christians follow various rules about what they can eat and how they should behave

lynched
illegally killed

mythical
derived from an ancient story

Satanic
extremely evil

secluded
lonely or isolated

shapeshifting
able to change form, for example, from a human into a wolf

trait
a feature or quality of something

transformed
changed into a different form

wracked
full of pain

Equipment

Never skimp on your werewolf-hunting equipment: it is always worth spending the maximum possible on it. After all, one day your life might depend on it!

Silver weapons
Always check if there is a hallmark (a mark stamped into a real silver item) to make sure they really are silver. You don't want to discover just as a werewolf closes in that they're only PART silver, and don't work.

Used bullets tend not to be available, but other secondhand weapons will be fine. Never buy secondhand unless you can meet the previous owner—though if they're dead, it might be a sign that the weapons don't work all that well.

Herbs, potions, etc.
Always buy these as fresh as possible.

Ideally, get your supplies in the area where the werewolf you are hunting lives. That way, everything will be suited to fighting the local werewolf population.

More Werewolf Information

Other Books

A Practical Guide To Vampires Werewolves, and Other Shapeshifters Anita Ganeri (Wayland, 2010) Contains basic information about werewolves and other shapeshifting monsters from around the world.

Tales Of Horror: Werewolves Jim Pipe (Ticktock Media, 2006) A great collection of rollicking werewolf stories, guaranteed to have you hiding under the covers at night!

Wolf Man Susan Gates (Usborne Publishing, 2009) A rollercoaster ride of an adventure story, this book is a mystery with a strange, supernatural twist.

The Internet

www.monstropedia.org This is a great, big rambling site that is absolutely full of information about all kinds of weird, supernatural, and scary creatures. To get to the werewolves section, click on "Shapeshifters," then "Werewolves."

www.werewolves.com All kinds of information is found on this site: news about forthcoming werewolf movies; tales of werewolves from hundreds of years ago; or light-hearted articles about Things You Could Get Away With If You Were A Werewolf ("Always win the prize for Best Costume at Halloween parties"…).

Movies and DVDs

Check the werewolves.com website at http://www.werewolves.com/ werewolf-movies-to-watch-out-for/ for forthcoming werewolf movies. Here are some classics, both old and new:

The Wolfman (1941, dir. George Waggner) The all-time classic werewolf movie. The script was influenced by writer Curt Siodmak's experiences in Nazi Germany before World War II.

The Howling (1981, dir. Joe Dante) From the director of *Gremlins*, this is a much darker, scarier movie. A reporter and her husband decide to take a vacation in a lonely village. There's just one problem: it's home to a community of werewolves.

Dog Soldiers (2002, dir. Neil Marshall) A group of soldiers out on patrol in the wilds of Scotland find themselves under attack by a family of werewolves. They take shelter in a lonely farmhouse; but all is not what it seems… Will any of them survive the night?

Note to parents and teachers: every effort has been made by the Publishers to ensure that these web sites are suitable for children, that they are of the highest educational value, and that they contain no inappropriate or offensive material. However, because of the nature of the Internet, it is impossible to guarantee that the contents of these sites will not be altered. We strongly advise that Internet access is supervised by a responsible adult.

Index

Amarok 21

Beast, the 20–21
Benandanti 24–25
Brazil 22, 23

Catholics 19

France 14, 15
full moon 4, 6, 7, 13, 19, 20, 23

Gandillon family 14–15
Goatman 28

Iceland 8, 9
Italy 24

Jura Mountains 14, 15

Latvia 12, 13
Lithuania 12, 13
lobisomem 22–23

Malandanti 24
Momo 29
Monkey Man 29
movies 4, 11, 23, 26–27, 28

Native Americans 16, 17, 21, 27

pricolici 10–11
protective plants 5, 17

Romania 10, 11
rougarou 18–19

Scandinavia 8
shapeshifters 4, 17, 27
Shunka wara'kin 21
Sigmund 8–9
silver bullets and weapons 4, 7, 11, 23
Sinfjotli 8–9
skinwalkers 16–17, 21

The Underworld 27

This edition first published in 2012 by

Sea-to-Sea Publications
Distributed by Black Rabbit Books
P.O. Box 3263, Mankato, Minnesota 56002

Copyright © Sea-to-Sea Publications 2012

Printed in China

All rights reserved.

9 8 7 6 5 4 3 2

Published by arrangement with the
Watts Publishing Group Ltd, London.

Series editors: Adrian Cole and Julia Bird
Art director: Jonathan Hair
Design: Mayer Media
Picture research: Diana Morris

A CIP catalog record for this book
is available from the Library of Congress.

ISBN: 978-1-59771-318-4

February 2011
RD/6000006415/001

Acknowledgements:
Alhovik/Shutterstock: 4-5 b/g. Arfey/Shutterstock: 20br.
The Art Archive/Alamy: 24b. Marilyn Barbone/Shutterstock:
30bl, 5brt. Stephane Bidouze/Shutterstock: 11b.
www.bigearthpublishing.com. Artwork by Jeff Easley: 20bl.
Blueberg/Alamy: 22t. © 2010 The British Library, London: 5t.
Jackie Carvey/Shutterstock: 2c. Hal D Crawford from" The
Aliens", 1970, Crawford, Hayden Hewes and Kietha Hewes:
29tl. Sergei Devyatkin/Shutterstock: 5br, 30tr.
DLILLC/Corbis: 12bl. Terrance Emerson/Shutterstock: 19t.
Everett Collection/Rex Features: 4t. Fabio Fersa/Shutterstock:
4bl. Fortean PL/Topfoto: 9t. The Granger Collection/
Topfoto: 15bl. Eric Isselée/Shutterstock: 18b. Amy Johansson/
Shutterstock: 11tl, 23b, 27c. jumping sack/Shutterstock: 13r.
Kojot/Shutterstock: 6b, 7c, 13bl, 15br, 17tr, 19b, 25b, 28tr.
© Lions Gate/Everett Collection/Rex Features: 16b.
© Lee Luker: 28b. Natalia Lukiyanova/frenta/Shutterstock:
3tr, 8t, 10t, 12c, 14t, 16tr, 18c, 20tr, 22b, 24c. Ing. Schieder
Markus/Shutterstock: 8b. Moviestore Collection Ltd/Alamy:
27b. Nyord/Shutterstock: 23t. Photos12/Alamy: 21, 26.
Picturepartners/Shutterstock: 5bl. Jean-Pierre Pieuchot/
Getty Images: 14b. Scott Rothstein/Shutterstock: 4bc, 12tl,
16tl, 20tl, 24tl, 28tl. Roberto A Sanchez/istockphoto: 29br.
Elzbieta Sekowska /Shutterstock: 17tc. Porojinicu Stellan/
Shutterstock: 10b. Tom Tietz/istockphoto: 17b.
Trent/Fotolia: front cover. Universal/Everett Collection/Rex
Features: 7t. www.vafis.info: 11t. Anthony Wallis/Fortean PL/
Topfoto: 25t. Igor Xill/Shutterstock: 6c.